D1313297

Join the **Rainbow Magic Reading Challenge!**

Read the story and collect your fairy points to climb the
Reading Rainbow at the back of the book.

To Isla, Lara and Maggie

Special thanks to
Rachel Elliot

ORCHARD BOOKS

First published in Great Britain in 2022 by The Watts Publishing Group

1 3 5 7 9 10 8 6 4 2

© 2022 Rainbow Magic Limited.
© 2022 HIT Entertainment Limited.
Illustrations © 2022 The Watts Publishing Group Limited.

HiT entertainment

A CIP catalogue record for this book is available from the British Library.

ISBN 978 1 40836 462 8

Printed and bound in Great Britain by Clays Ltd, Elcograf S.p.A

MIX
Paper from
responsible sources
FSC® C104740
www.fsc.org

The paper and board used in this book are made from wood from responsible sources.

Orchard Books
An imprint of Hachette Children's Group
Part of The Watts Publishing Group Limited
Carmelite House, 50 Victoria Embankment, London EC4Y 0DZ

An Hachette UK Company
www.hachette.co.uk
www.hachettechildrens.co.uk

Seren
the Sausage Dog Fairy

By Daisy Meadows

ORCHARD

www.orchardseriesbooks.co.uk

Jack Frost's Ode

Puppy care sounds dull and dreary.
Training rules just make me weary.
These fairies must be made to see
No puppy matters more than me!

The fairies dared to tell me "no",
So far away their pups will go.
And if they don't do what I say,
I'll yell at them till they obey!

Contents

Chapter One
Tippington Pet Shop

"I think this might actually be the best shop in the world," said Kirsty Tate.

She turned slowly on the spot, smiling at shelves lined with pet toys, collars and leads; tanks teeming with jewel-bright fish; and pens filled with fluffy rabbits and guinea pigs. Her best friend, Rachel

Walker, ran her hand over a pile of soft
puppy bedding.

"Buttons loves it in here," she said.
"Most shops don't let dogs in, but here
they always make a fuss of him."

Kirsty darted over to a display of tiny
velvet cat collars.

"These would look so cute on Pearl,"
she said, running her fingers along the
row.

Rachel crouched down to look at some
dog treats. Then she shook her head and
stood up again.

"I could spend hours in here," she said.
"But we have to get on with our errand.
Nate is relying on us."

Nate was the manager of the Leafy
Lane Animal Shelter, where Rachel
and Kirsty were volunteering for a few

days. The shelter had rescued a litter of tiny newborn puppies, and Nate needed lots of help. He had given them a list of things to buy from the pet shop. Kirsty took it out of her pocket and read aloud.

"Five puppy collars," she said. "One pack of puppy pads, one puppy comb, one pack of puppy milk formula—"

"Not so fast!" said Rachel, who was pushing the shopping trolley. "I'm still looking at the collars."

Kirsty giggled and came over to help pick five colourful collars for the white puppies at the shelter.

"Red, yellow, pink, green and blue," she said as she dropped them into the trolley. "They'll look like a little rainbow."

Soon the trolley was filled with puppy supplies.

"And last of all, a jumbo pack of sanitising wipes," said Rachel, adding them to the pile. "Goodness, our arms will be aching after carrying all this back to the shelter."

Just then, they heard a great commotion. People were shouting, and dogs were barking and whining.

"What on earth is going on?" Kirsty asked.

They were near the back of the shop. When they walked to the end of the aisle, they saw a big archway with the words "Puppy Grooming Parlour" written in curly red letters. Under the arch were three uniformed puppy groomers, swarms of puppies and a crowd of owners.

The groomers and the owners were all shouting and waving their arms around.

And as for the puppies . . .

"Oh my goodness," said Kirsty, gasping.

There was a border collie whose silky coat had been curled into ringlets and decorated with at least a hundred red ribbons. A husky's coat had been gelled into spikes, and an unhappy-looking Pomeranian was modelling an eighties perm. There was a poodle whose curls had been straightened and an Afghan hound with a very wonky haircut.

"I'm so sorry," one of the groomers kept repeating. "I can't understand what's gone wrong today."

Rachel and Kirsty shared a worried glance. They knew exactly why the puppy grooming had been such a disaster. As well as volunteering at the shelter, they had been busy helping the Puppy Care Fairies. Naughty Jack Frost had stolen their puppies, as well as the enchanted collars that helped the fairies make their magic. The girls had helped to find Li the Labrador Fairy's puppy, Buddy, and Frenchie the Bulldog Fairy's puppy, Pepper, but two of the puppies were still missing.

"Until we find Wiggles and Cleo, everything to do with grooming and training will go wrong," said Rachel.

"Look at the state of my Japanese Akita," one woman wailed at the groomers. "He's gone blue!"

"I didn't want you to shave all her fur off!" a man was complaining, holding a Bichon Frise wrapped in a blanket.

"I wish we could help," said Kirsty.

"There's nothing we can do right now," said Rachel. "Let's go and pay."

Feeling downcast, the girls walked along the toy aisle towards the tills. As they passed a large bucket of chew toys, Kirsty stopped in her tracks.

"What is it?" Rachel asked.

Kirsty pointed at the bucket.

"That squishy octopus is glowing," she whispered.

Rachel checked left and right, but there was no one else in the aisle. Her fingers tingled with excitement as she picked up the blue octopus.

"Do you think it's magic?" she asked.

As if to answer her question, the glow grew brighter and the toy disappeared. In its place was a tiny glimmering fairy.

Chapter Two
Gossiping Bunnies

"Hi, remember me?" the fairy said in a merry voice. "I'm Seren the Sausage Dog Fairy."

"Of course we do," said Rachel at once. "Welcome to Tippington."

Everything about Seren seemed bouncy and bright, from her dark green

polka-flowered dress to her bobbed red hair. Her freckly nose scrunched up as she smiled at them.

"I'm so glad I found you," she exclaimed, jumping up and down on Rachel's hand and clapping her hands together. "I hoped and hoped that I'd find you in a quiet place so we could talk straight away."

"This isn't exactly quiet," said Kirsty, casting a nervous glance over her shoulder. "Shoppers could come down this aisle any minute."

"I'm sure they won't," said Seren.

She twirled over to a nearby shelf and landed on a rubber pig toy, which let out a loud *OINK*. Seren shot upwards again and squealed with laughter.

"Wiggles would love that!" she cried.

"I have to get him one. When he comes home, that is."

She sat down and her smile faded a little.

"Is there still no sign of him?" asked Rachel.

"No one has seen him," said Seren. "But I heard a rumour, and that's why I'm here."

"What sort of rumour?" Kirsty asked.

"I was feeling miserable this morning," said Seren. "I've searched everywhere, and I've asked everyone I know, but I haven't seen any sign of him. Not even a single paw print. I was starting to think that

maybe I would never find Wiggles."

Rachel hopped from one foot to the other in anticipation.

"I was sitting outside my toadstool cottage when a bunny hopped up to me," Seren went on. "He was holding a letter in his mouth, written on a piece of bark. It was from his snow hare cousin in the Ice Mountains."

"I didn't know that you could write on bark," said Kirsty.

"I didn't know that bunnies could write," said Rachel.

"The snow hare often writes to tell him about the silly things that the goblins do," said Seren. "Bunnies are such gossips. The latest news was that a goblin had set up a puppy grooming shop. He had sent out adverts to everyone in the mountains.

The snow hare didn't know about Wiggles, but as soon as the bunny got the letter, he thought of me."

"The goblin must have Wiggles," said Kirsty. "With the help of the magical collar, he could be the best puppy groomer in the world."

"Exactly," said Seren. "I have to find out if Wiggles is being kept prisoner in Goblin Grotto, but I don't know how to get there without being spotted. I have a feeling that I would stand out in the goblin village."

"We'll help you," said Rachel at once. "We've been there before. If that goblin has Wiggles, we'll rescue him."

"We have to get the magical collar back too," said Kirsty, thinking of the puppy grooming parlour. "Without it,

puppies everywhere are facing a really,
really bad hair day!"

"What shall we do with our trolley?"
asked Rachel. "I know that time will
stand still while we've gone, but it isn't
right to abandon it in the aisle."

"I've got this," said Seren.

She waved her wand, and there was a
flurry of sparkles as the girls and their
trolley shrank to fairy size. Rachel and
Kirsty were smaller than the chew toys
in the bucket, and their gossamer wings
shimmered under the shop's lights.

With another flick of her wand, Seren
lifted the trolley up to the highest shelf.
Rachel and Kirsty flew up with it, and
then pushed it behind a packet of puppy
pads.

"It'll be safe there whilst we're away,"

said Seren. "And as for us . . ."

She peeped over the edge of the shelf
and waved her wand in a circle. Instantly,
a sort of whirlpool appeared below them.
It was deep blue, but it glimmered with
fairy dust in every colour of the rainbow.

"Time to dive in to an adventure,"
Seren said, winking at Rachel and Kirsty.

Side by side, the three fairies took a
deep breath . . . and jumped.

Chapter Three
Doggy Disguises

The fairies twisted and tumbled through
the whirlpool.

"It's like we're going up, not down!"
Kirsty called out.

"All I can see is sparkles!" Rachel cried.

WHOOSH! They suddenly burst out
of the sparkles as if they had been fired

out of a cannon. *WHUMP!* They landed
in a soft, snowy bank overlooking Goblin
Grotto.

"Now that was fun," said Seren.

Brushing snow out of their eyes, the
fairies scrambled to the edge of the bank
and looked down at the goblin village. It
was bustling with activity.

"It must be market day," said Kirsty.

She pointed to a few bedraggled stalls
in the middle of the village. Crowds of
goblin grown-ups and children were

trudging through muddy slush, carrying bags and baskets.

The wooden huts dotted around had plumes of smoke curling from the chimneys.

"How are we going to search the village on such a busy day?" asked Seren.

"In disguise," said Rachel and Kirsty together.

They looked at each other and giggled.

"I've never disguised anyone as a goblin before," said Seren. "Sounds like fun!"

She tapped each of them with her wand and then let out a little squeal.

"It tickles!"

The fairies giggled at each other as their wings vanished, their skin turned green and their noses grew long and thin. Their shoes disappeared as their feet grew wide and hairy.

"Brr, no wonder the goblins make such a fuss about having cold feet," said Kirsty in a squawky goblin voice.

Seren waved her wand and wrapped each of them in a warm cloak, a bobble hat and a pair of thick wellies.

Keeping their heads down, Rachel, Kirsty and Seren tramped down the snowy hill and into the village. The narrow street wound around higgledy-piggledy huts, and they passed many groups of goblins on the way. Several of them stared at Seren.

"Why are they looking at me?" asked Seren.

Rachel glanced at her.

"You're smiling," she said in a low voice. "Goblins have a natural scowl."

Seren rearranged her face into a grumpy expression, and the passing goblins stopped staring.

"That's weird," whispered Kirsty. "Did you see? That goblin who just went past was carrying a hen."

"What's so weird about a hen?" asked

Rachel, tilting her head to one side.

"It was dressed up as a dog," said Kirsty.

Rachel couldn't stop a sudden burst of laughter.

"Are you sure?" she said.

"I'm certain," said Kirsty. "It had fake ears and a collar."

"That's odd," said Seren.

"Well, Goblin Grotto is an odd place," said Kirsty.

A few steps further on, they saw a very small goblin struggling to carry a very large pig. It was wearing a cardboard

dog snout, held on by elastic.

"Stranger and stranger," said Rachel.

The further they walked, the more animals they saw in disguise. There were rats and weasels, geese and goats. There was even a very irritable Arctic fox. And every single one was dressed up as a dog.

"What is going on?" asked Kirsty, after they had passed a badger in a pink dog harness. "This is weird, even for the goblins."

"We'll have to ask," said Rachel.

A mother was coming towards them with a gaggle of naughty young goblins.

"Excuse me," said Kirsty, before remembering that goblins were never that polite. "I mean, hey you. Why are all these animals disguised as dogs?"

"Are you daft?" snapped the goblin

mother as one of her children swung on her headscarf. "Everyone wants to try the puppy groomer."

"But shouldn't they be taking their puppies to him?" asked Kirsty.

"There aren't any puppies around here, silly," said the mother. "But that's not going to stop us!"

"Where is he?" Rachel asked.

"Down that alley," said the goblin, jerking her thumb over shoulder. "Now leave me alone."

She walked on, dragging her children with her, and the fairies shared excited glances.

"We've found him," Seren whispered.

They went down the little alleyway in single file. After a few steps, they reached a queue of goblins outside a tumbledown hut. Each one of them was holding an animal, but there wasn't a single puppy in sight.

"Ducks, rabbits, squirrels," said Kirsty under her breath. "Goodness, is that a penguin?"

"Clear off," one of the goblins squawked at them. "No dog, no place."

"I've got an idea," said Rachel.

She slipped around a corner and took off her cloak. Then she bundled it up as if she had a dog wrapped up inside.

"Now we can join the queue," she said.

Chapter Four
The Vanishing Goblin

"Next!" squawked a grumpy voice.

"Thank goodness," said Rachel.

Her arms were aching from pretending to hold a dog in the same position for so long. But at last, a goblin in a smart pink uniform was scowling at them from the doorway of the hut. The words

"Gorgeous Goblin Grooming" were printed on the uniform in swirly gold lettering.

She walked into the hut with Seren and Kirsty close behind her. Inside, a goblin was standing in the middle of the hut wearing the same pink uniform. He was holding a shaver in one hand and a nail clipper in the other. A brush and a comb were dangling from his belt.

"What's that?" he asked nastily, looking at the bundle in Rachel's arms.

Rachel shook out the cloak as Kirsty shut the door. Seren waved her wand and their goblin disguises melted away. The goblin gaped at their fairy wings.

"Get away from me!" he screeched.

"We just want to—"

"No!"

He snatched up a rucksack from a chair, yanked the door open and fled into the street. There was no time for another magical disguise. The fairies zoomed after him, swooping into the air to follow the running pink figure. His rucksack bobbed up and down on his back as he ran.

"Did you hear a yap?" said Seren.

Suddenly, a little brown head poked out of the top of the rucksack. Two silky ears

pricked up and a little nose wiggled.

"Wiggles!" Seren cried.

She zoomed along even faster, but the goblin darted sideways into another alleyway. Rachel and Kirsty swerved and saw him hurtle into one of the huts.

"In there!" Rachel called out, diving towards the hut.

"We've got him," said Kirsty.

The fairies landed outside and Seren pelted in, ready to pull her precious puppy away from the goblin. But she skidded to a halt on a rug in the middle of the room.

It was completely empty.

"But . . . but that's impossible," Seren stammered. "We saw him come in here."

"Goblins can't just vanish," said Rachel.

"Maybe Jack Frost gave him enough

magic to get to the Ice Castle," said
Kirsty. "He's done it before."

"But surely the goblin would have used
the magic as soon as he saw us," said
Rachel.

The three fairies stared at each other.

"The windows," said Seren. "Perhaps he
climbed out that way."

But the windows were locked on the
inside. There was nothing inside the
room except the rug on which Seren
had skidded. The Sausage Dog Fairy's
shoulders slumped.

"Somehow, he's got away," she said. "I
feel as if I've lost Wiggles all over again."

Feeling helpless, Kirsty bent down to
straighten the rucked-up rug.

"That's strange," she said. "It's caught
on something."

She tugged on the rug, but it didn't move. She tugged again and it still didn't move.

"Try lifting it up," said Rachel.

Kirsty pulled it upwards.

"It's heavy," she said, panting. "Help me."

Together, all three of them pulled the rug.

"It's coming!" Seren exclaimed.

The rug gave way, there was a loud *CRASH* and the fairies fell backwards. Where the rug had been was a square hole in the floor.

"It's a trapdoor," said Kirsty, amazed. "The rug is attached to it, so it flaps into place when the trapdoor shuts."

They peered into the dark hole. It was too narrow for them to be able to fly.

Stone steps led downwards, fading into blackness below.

"Where do you think it leads?" Rachel asked.

Her voice was echoed back at her from the hole. "Leads . . . leads . . . leads . . ."

"There's only one way to find out," said Seren. "Adventure, here we come."

Chapter Five
Where the Tunnel Went

Deeper, deeper, deeper the fairies went.
Their footsteps echoed around them, and
Kirsty counted seventeen steps before
they reached the bottom.

"What is it?" Rachel whispered.
"Where are we?"

Seren held up her wand and tiny

bubbles of pure light burst from it. Each
bubble floated upwards and attached
itself to the ceiling of a narrow tunnel.
It wound away from them in both
directions.

"Shall we go left or right?" Seren asked.
"They both look the same."

"Wait," said Kirsty, peering at the dark
ground. "What's that?"

Something was
glimmering a little
way down the
left-hand tunnel.
Seren sent another
bubble of light
towards the ground,
and it lit up a tiny
silver dog tag in the
shape of a comb.

"That belongs to Wiggles," said Seren, rushing to pick it up. "It's from his collar."

"This must be the way that the goblin went," said Rachel. "It was lucky that the tag fell off."

"That wasn't luck," said Seren as they set off down the tunnel. "That was Wiggles. He's such a clever boy. He pulled it off and dropped it because he knew that we would find it."

The tunnel was cold and long. In the light from the bubbles, the fairies could see their breath in the air. After several minutes, the tunnel opened up and became a round chamber of stone. There was an open door on the other side.

"I can see steps," said Kirsty, fluttering forwards.

Again, the space was too narrow for

them to fly. They tiptoed up in single file, shivering.

"I never knew that there were tunnels under Goblin Grotto," said Rachel. "Where do you think we are?"

"It's getting colder," Seren whispered. "Wherever we are, it's like ice."

There was a distant rumble above their heads.

"Is that thunder?" asked Kirsty.

They took a few more steps and heard a squawk.

"That's a goblin," said Rachel. "And the rumble isn't thunder – it's running feet."

They could hear yells and footsteps now. Water was dripping somewhere nearby.

"I feel as if we've been here before," said Kirsty.

"We have!" Rachel exclaimed suddenly. "Kirsty, we're in the dungeons of the Ice Castle."

Seren gasped and staggered sideways against the stone wall. She had gone very pale.

"The Ice Castle?" she whispered. "What if Jack Frost hears us?"

"Keep going," said Kirsty, squeezing her hand. "We have to try."

"I can't move," said Seren. "I'm scared."

Rachel took Seren's other hand.

"We understand," she said. "We've been here lots of times and we still get scared. But Wiggles needs us."

Just then they heard barking and scampering feet. Seren looked up.

"That's Wiggles," she said in a stronger voice. "He must have escaped. He's

leading the goblins a merry dance all
around the castle."

"That sounds like something we ought
to see," said Kirsty with a little smile.

After a few more steps, they reached
another door and Rachel peeped around
it.

"It leads into a corridor," she whispered.
"There's a pile of broken furniture we
could hide behind."

They slipped through the door and
crouched down behind cobwebby three-
legged chairs, ripped paintings and
cracked tables. Seren peered at the picture
nearest to her and shuddered.

"Who's that?" she asked.

The figure in the portrait had the same
spiky hair and sour expression as Jack
Frost. Rachel and Kirsty recognised her

at once.

"That's Jilly
Chilly," said Kirsty.
"Jack Frost's little
sister."

Seren's eyes
opened wide in
surprise, but just
then they heard
running feet and
Wiggles shot past
their hiding place
with a wand in his mouth. Seconds
later, the pink-uniformed goblin came
staggering after him.

"Stop – right – there," he panted,
clutching his side. "I've got a – stitch."

There was a loud *WOOF*, and Wiggles
zoomed through his legs and raced in

the opposite direction. With a groan, the
goblin followed him.

"This is a game Wiggles loves to play,"
said Seren. "He'll race around until
everyone except him is exhausted and
then fall asleep chewing whatever he's
stolen."

"Maybe we can get him to notice us
and come this way," said Rachel.

She and Kirsty giggled as Wiggles skidded past them, tumbled over his own feet, did a somersault and then kept on running. The goblin followed again.

Suddenly, a bony hand shot out of nowhere and snatched the goblin almost off his feet. Seren gasped and clapped both hands over her mouth.

It was Jack Frost!

Chapter Six
A Puppy and a Portrait

"Why have I been woken from my nap?" Jack Frost hissed at the goblin. "Where is my wand? And what is all that dratted yapping?"

"It's my puppy," the goblin wailed.

Jack Frost shook him.

"What do you mean, 'your' puppy?"

he growled. "All the puppies are my puppies!"

Wiggle scampered past again, and Seren dared to peep out from behind the portrait.

"I'm sorry, but I had to come," the goblin gabbled. "There were f—"

"I ordered you not to bring that hound here till it was trained," Jack Frost yelled. "I've just trodden in three separate puddles!"

Wiggles stopped to chase his own tail and Seren beckoned to him again, but he didn't see her.

"I'm sorry," the goblin squawked again. "But these fai—"

"I don't care how hard the training is, you nincompoop," Jack Frost bellowed. "I'm far too busy to be dealing with a

nasty, yappy, wand-chewing puppy. I need my beauty sleep!"

At that moment the goblin spotted Seren leaning out from behind Jilly Chilly's portrait.

"F–fair–fair–" he stammered, pointing at her.

"Stop interrupting me!" Jack Frost shrieked.

Wiggles spotted Seren, dropped the wand and scampered towards her.

"Fairies!" the goblin blurted out.

Jack Frost grabbed at Wiggles, who dodged out of his grasp, tumbled sideways and slid into Seren's open arms.

"I've got you!" she gasped, staggering backwards.

Rachel and Kirsty pulled her towards the nearest window as Jack Frost

floundered across the broken furniture.

"Come back here with my puppy!" he roared.

Kirsty struggled with the window catch.

"Quickly!" Rachel exclaimed.

Jack Frost lunged at them as the catch turned. Kirsty flung open the window and the fairies flew out with Wiggles. They turned and saw Jack Frost sitting among the shattered chairs and tables.

His head had broken through the portrait of his sister and he was wearing it like a collar.

"You'll be sorry!" he yelled, shaking his fist.

Joyfully, Rachel, Kirsty, Seren and Wiggles zoomed into the air and flew away from the icy battlements.

"We did it," said Seren, high-fiving Kirsty. "I can't believe we did it!"

She clipped
the silver comb
tag back on to
Wiggles's magical
yellow collar.

"I have the
yummiest dinner
ever waiting at
home for you," she
said, kissing his silky little head.

Rachel and Kirsty stroked Wiggles and
tickled his ears. He opened his mouth in
a sort of puppy smile.

"Now puppies everywhere are safe
from grim grooms," said Rachel, with
a laugh. "And best of all, Wiggles is safe
again."

"Thank you for everything," said Seren,
smiling at them both. "I think it's time

for you to go back to the pet shop. Those little puppies at the shelter need you too."

"Goodbye," said Kirsty, giving Wiggles a final pat. "I hope we see you again soon."

"Me too," said Seren.

She waved her wand, and her face faded until all they could see was sparkling fairy dust. They blinked and found themselves back in the toy aisle of the pet shop. They wings had disappeared, and they were human again.

"Here comes our trolley," said Rachel.

It was floating down from the top shelf, growing bigger as it came. When it landed next to them, it was back to its normal size.

"Wow," said Kirsty, letting out a sigh of relief. "That was a whirlwind adventure."

There was a deep woof behind them, and the border collie they had seen earlier walked past with his owner. His ringlets and ribbons had gone, and his coat was silky and smart.

"It looks as if everything is back to normal here as well," said Rachel, smiling as she spotted the fluffy Pomeranian, now perm-free. "Thank goodness."

"Let's take these things to the shelter," said Kirsty. "It must be time for the puppies to have their next feed . . . and their next cuddle."

They headed towards the tills, enjoying spotting each dog they had seen earlier, now beautifully groomed. As they joined the queue, they saw a poodle trotting past proudly, its tail in the air.

"Pandora the Poodle Fairy still needs

our help," said Rachel. "I hope we'll meet her again soon."

"Me too," said Kirsty, linking arms with her best friend. "Because I can't wait for our next adventure!"

The End

Now it's time for Kirsty and
Rachel to help...

Pandora the Poodle Fairy

Read on for a sneak peek...

"Buttons, fetch!" Rachel Walker called.

Her Old English Sheepdog bounded
across the park after his ball, which
splashed into the stream. Buttons took a
flying leap into the water.

"Doggy belly-flop!" exclaimed Rachel's
best friend, Kirsty Tate. "Oh no, Buttons,
don't come near me."

But the dog splashed out of the stream,
soggy and muddy, and bounded over
to drop the ball at Kirsty's feet. Then
he shook his shaggy coat, and the girls
squealed as they were splattered in icy
brown water.

"Oh Buttons, we're going to have to change our clothes before we go to the shelter," said Rachel, laughing ruefully. "I look as if I've been jumping in the stream."

The girls had been volunteering at the Leafy Lane Animal Shelter all half term, looking after some newborn puppies that needed special care.

"I thought it was only puppies who were full of bounce," said Kirsty as Rachel clipped on Buttons's lead.

"Buttons always bounces when he sees a stream," said Rachel, laughing. "Come on, let's go back to my house and get changed."

The girls had been spending a lot of time around puppies lately. As well as their volunteer work at the shelter, they had been on a magical adventure with some new fairy friends. Li the Labrador Fairy had invited them to the Puppy Care Fair in Fairyland. Everything had gone wrong when Jack Frost had demanded a puppy before he knew how to look after one. When the Puppy Care Fairies said no, he stole their four puppies and magical collars and hid them.

"I keep expecting Pandora the Poodle Fairy to appear at any minute," said Kirsty as they walked back through the park. "Cleo is the only puppy still missing."

"We found all the others," said Rachel, holding on tightly to Buttons's lead. "I know we can find Cleo too. Stop pulling so hard, Buttons."

"I hope we do see Pandora soon," said

Kirsty. "She must be worried. Oh!"

She almost fell over as Buttons darted across the path in front of her.

"Sorry," said Rachel, pulling him back. "It's as if he's forgotten things he's known since he was a puppy."

"I expect it's because Cleo is missing," said Kirsty. "After all, Pandora looks after puppy training. Perhaps older dogs will start to lose their puppy training memories."

Buttons let out a loud woof and dashed forwards, jerking the lead out of Rachel's hand. He hurtled along the path and jumped up at a man who was walking towards them.

"I'm really sorry," said Rachel, hurrying over to him. "Oh, hello Carl!"

The man smiled at both girls over a

bundle of blankets in his arms.

"Carl helped us to train Buttons when he was a puppy," said Rachel. "Carl, this is my best friend, Kirsty."

"Hello, Kirsty," said Carl. "Great to see you again, Rachel. How is the lovely Buttons getting on?"

"He's fine, thanks," said Rachel, picking up the lead again. "He's being a bit cheeky this morning but he's usually really good."

"It seems to be that sort of day," said Car,l with a grin. "My early-morning puppy training class was a disaster. The owners had forgotten everything and the puppies wouldn't even listen to me."

Rachel and Kirsty shared a hurried glance. They knew exactly why puppy training classes were going wrong.

"I hope things will be better at your next class," said Rachel.

"Thanks," Carl replied with a smile. "I'm on my way to the Leafy Lane Animal Shelter."

"Us too," said Rachel in surprise. "We're volunteering for half term."

"Ah, the newborn puppies," said Carl, nodding. "I heard that the manager had asked for more volunteers. I help out there once a week, advising the manager about what sort of families the animals will suit."

"It'll be interesting to watch you work," said Rachel. "We just have to take Buttons home first."

"I've got some extra work for the manager this morning," said Carl. "Look what I found."

He folded back the edge of the blanket he was carrying, and a huge pair of trusting eyes looked up at the girls. A little pink tongue licked Carl's hand.

"She's a friendly young lady," Carl said.

The little dog's eyes were gunky, and her coat was matted with leaves and mud.

"Poor little thing," said Kirsty, gently stroking her head.

"Maybe you two could help to clean her up," Carl suggested.

"We'd love to," said Rachel. "Come on, Buttons, Kirsty and I have got work to do!"

When Rachel and Kirsty arrived at the shelter, they went straight to the kennel where the newborn puppies were sleeping. There was a lot to do. The girls started by feeding them with milk substitute. Then the puppies needed to be burped and helped to go to the toilet.

As soon as the litter was sleeping peacefully, the girls went to find Nate, the manager. He was in the garden behind the shelter, watching Carl work with a greyhound who had been left at the shelter the day before. Several older dogs were sniffing around the grass, and the puppy that Carl had found was finishing a bowl of food beside him.

"We've fed the puppies and put the dirty towels and blankets in the washing machine," said Kirsty. "What would you like us to do next?"

Nate smiled down at her.

"That's great work," he said. "I believe you've already met our newest arrival. We've fed her, but she needs to be washed and groomed. Would you be able to do that?"

"We'd love to," said Kirsty.

"I've bathed Buttons lots of times," Rachel added.

Nate showed them an old tin bath filled with warm water. Beside it was a soft puppy bed, a bottle of dog shampoo, a thick towel, a comb and some pet wipes. A hose lay on the grass beside them.

"Make sure you dry her really well afterwards," he said. "The sunshine will do the rest."

He went to help Carl, and the girls carefully placed the dirty puppy into the water. She stood still as they massaged shampoo through her tangled coat.

"She's so sweet," said Rachel. "I think she knows that we're trying to help her."

Slowly, the water in the bath became darker. Kirsty picked up the hose and turned on a gentle spray of warm water.

"I'll rinse her face by hand while you do her body," said Rachel.

"It looks as if she's chocolate brown," said Kirsty after a few moments. "It was hard to tell before."

"I'm sure I've met her," Rachel said. "Maybe I've seen her with her owner in the park."

"She looks familiar to me too," said Kirsty. "Do you think she's a poodle?"

" know who she reminds me of," said Rachel suddenly. "She looks just like Cleo."

The girls stared at one another and then back at the puppy. Could this really be Pandora's magical puppy? They had seen her a few days ago at the Puppy Care Fair, but they hadn't met her close up.

"Is it possible?" whispered Kirsty.

Rachel lifted the puppy out of the bath and wrapped her in the towel.

"Cleo?" she said.

The dog looked up at her eagerly and let out a little yip.

"I'm sure it's her," said Rachel, tingling with surprise and excitement. "This is wonderful! Now all we have to do is take her back to Pandora and everything will go back to normal."

"But how are we going to get her to Fairyland?" asked Kirsty, glancing around at Carl and Nate. "We can't use our fairy dust in front of them. They would be sure to notice."

During their adventures with the Weather Fairies, the girls had each been given a special locket by Queen Titania. There was just enough fairy dust inside each one for a trip to Fairyland.

Wondering what to do next, the girls combed Cleo's silky coat and used the wipes to clean her ears. As they were checking her paws, Carl's voice carried over the grass to them.

"Remember, distract him from behaviour you don't like," he was telling Nate. "Use a toy to get his attention and play with him."

"That's it," said Rachel. "We need a distraction."

She still had a pocket full of dog treats from their walk with Buttons. Giving Cleo to Kirsty, she took a big handful of treats and made sure that the older dogs in the garden could see her. They came running over. Nate and Carl still weren't looking.

"Now," Kirsty whispered.

Rachel threw the treats to the far side of the garden as hard as she could. There was instant and total pandemonium as all the dogs belted across the garden. Woofing and yipping, they zoomed past Carl and Nate and nearly knocked them down.

"What's the matter with them?" Nate asked.

"We'd better go and check," said Carl. As the men jogged after the dogs,

Rachel and Kirsty wrapped their arms around Cleo and opened their lockets. A helpful breeze blew the fairy dust over them, and they shrank to fairy size at once.

"Find Pandora," said Rachel.

Cleo whined.

"Don't worry," Kirsty whispered in Cleo's ear. "We're taking you home."

There was a burst of sparkling stars all around, as dazzling as fireworks. Every colour of the rainbow danced before their eyes. They clung together as they whirled away from the human world.

Cleo whined in alarm as the sparkles and stars grew more vibrant. Then, in the blink of an eye, they were standing

in a little meadow filled with lush
green grass. They fluttered their gauzy
wings and shared a smile of breathless
happiness.

"We're back in Fairyland," said Rachel.

"But where in Fairyland?" Kirsty
wondered. "Do you think we've come to
the right place?"

them, and the girls peeped inside.

**Read Pandora the Poodle Fairy to
find out what adventures are in store for Kirsty and Rachel!**